Who Will Win the Cup?

by **Elizabeth Dale**

illustrated by **Sophie Foster**

It is a big day for the elephants and rhinos...

V

It is the football cup!

"We will win!" yell the elephants.

"We will win!" yell the rhinos.

The referee yells, "Go!"

The rhinos kick the ball.

The elephants stop the ball.

They run with it to the rhino's goal.

9

They shoot.

The rhino jumps.

"Goal!" yell the elephants. "Yippee!"

The big rhino kicks the ball to the small rhino.

She kicks it back.

The big rhino shoots.

The elephant stops the ball.

The rhinos shoot again.

The elephant stops it.

17

"It's not fair!" yell all the rhinos.

The elephants kick the ball and run.

They shoot.

The rhino heads the ball...

...and keeps it!

The rhino runs past all the elephants...

... into the goal.

"Goal!" yell the rhinos.

"It's not fair!" yell all the elephants.

"You all win the cup!" yells the referee.

"Yippee!" yell the rhinos and elephants.

Quiz

1. What are the elephants and rhinos playing?
a) Tennis
b) Football
c) Cricket

2. What animal is the referee?
a) A monkey
b) A giraffe
c) A lion

3. What does the referee shout to start the game?
a) Start!
b) Go!
c) Run!

4. When the rhino heads the ball...
a) It bounces off
b) It rolls away
c) It gets stuck on his horn

5. Who wins the football cup?
a) The elephants
b) The rhinos
c) The elephants and the rhinos

Turn over for answers

Book Bands for Guided Reading

The Institute of Education book banding system is a scale of colours that reflects the various levels of reading difficulty. The bands are assigned by taking into account the content, the language style, the layout and phonics.

Maverick Early Readers are a bright, attractive range of books covering the pink to purple bands. All of these books have been book banded for guided reading to the industry standard and edited by a leading educational consultant.

To view the whole Maverick Readers scheme, visit our website at

www.maverickearlyreaders.com

Or scan the QR code above to view our scheme instantly!

Quiz Answers: 1b, 2a, 3b, 4c, 5c